DINOFOURS

WE LOVE MUD!

To Edie Weinberg,
thanks for everything!
—S.M.

Text copyright © 2003 by Scholastic Inc.
Illustrations copyright © 2003 by Hans Wilhelm, Inc.
All rights reserved. Published by Scholastic Inc.
SCHOLASTIC, CARTWHEEL BOOKS, DINOFOURS, and associated logos
are trademarks and/or registered trademarks of Scholastic Inc.

Library of Congress Cataloging-in-Publication Data

Metzger, Steve.
        We love mud! / by Steve Metzger ; illustrations by Hans Wilhelm.
            p. cm. — (Dinofours)
        "Cartwheel Books."
        Summary: Danielle overcomes her dislike of getting dirty and joins the other Dinofours in playing in the mud.
        ISBN 0-439-38220-3 (pbk. : alk. paper)
            [1. Mud--Fiction. 2. Cleanliness — Fiction. 3. Nursery schools — Fiction. 4. Schools — Fiction. 5. Dinosaurs — Fiction.]
    I. Wilhelm, Hans, 1945-ill. II. Title.

    PZ7.M56775 We 2003
    [E]--dc21   2002007237

10 9 8 7 6 5 4 3   03 04 05 06 07

                                    Printed in the U.S.A.   24
                                First printing, March 2003

DINOFOURS®

WE LOVE MUD!

by Steve Metzger
Illustrated by Hans Wilhelm

Cartwheel
·B·O·O·K·S·®

SCHOLASTIC INC.
New York   Toronto   London   Auckland   Sydney
Mexico City   New Delhi   Hong Kong   Buenos Aires

It had rained all night long. The next morning, Danielle and her mother walked to school.

"Look, Mommy!" said Danielle. "Everything is so wet!"

"Watch where you're walking," said Danielle's mother. "You might step in a puddle and get muddy feet."

"I won't," said Danielle, looking down. "I'll be careful."

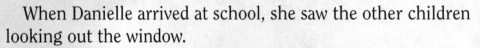

When Danielle arrived at school, she saw the other children looking out the window.

"I can't wait to go outside!" said Albert. "I'm going to jump in every puddle."

"I love puddles!" said Brendan. "One day I jumped in a puddle so many times my mommy called me a jumping bean!"

"Look at our dirt pit!" called Tara. "Now it's a mud pit!"

"Wow!" said Joshua.

Turning to Danielle, Tracy said, "I love mud! Do *you*?"
"No!" Danielle replied. "I don't like to get dirty."
"Why not?" asked Joshua.
"I just don't!" said Danielle as she stomped off.

Sitting in her cubby, Danielle sang this song:

Dirty mud! Messy mud!
Dry up and go away.
I do not like you, muddy mud.
That's all I have to say!

Mrs. Dee walked over to Danielle.

"What's the matter?" asked Mrs. Dee. "Why aren't you having fun with the other children?"

"I'm in a bad mood," said Danielle. "Everyone wants to play in the mud...but not me."

"Why don't you like mud?" asked Mrs. Dee. "When I was a little girl, I loved playing in the mud."

"I don't like to get dirty," replied Danielle.

"That's all right," said Mrs. Dee. "You don't have to play in the mud if you don't want to."

"Okay!" said Danielle as she looked up. "I'll go play on the swings, and then I won't get messy at all."

Later that morning, it was time to play outside. Mrs. Dee opened the door and the Dinofours raced to the playground.

Tara, Tracy, and Joshua skipped over to the muddy dirt pit and started to make mud pies. Albert and Brendan ran to the biggest puddle they could find and jumped up and down in it.

Danielle went straight to the swings. As she began swinging back and forth, she watched Tara, Tracy, and Joshua playing their muddy game.

"I'm making a flat mud pie for Mrs. Dee," said Tara.

"I'm making a round mud pie for my mommy," said Tracy.

"And I'm going to make a birthday mud pie for my daddy," said Joshua.

"That's a great idea!" said Tara. "Let's get sticks and pretend they're candles."

Danielle watched as Tara, Tracy, and Joshua gathered the stick candles and put them in Joshua's mud pie. Soon, she began to wish that she was playing with them, too. Then Danielle looked at Brendan and Albert.

"Look at the water splashing everywhere!" said Brendan as he jumped up and down in the puddle.

"I'm jumping so high," said Albert. "I can almost touch the sky!"

Danielle smiled as she looked at Albert and Brendan. *That looks like fun,* she thought.

After a few more jumps, Brendan said, "Hey, old buddy. Let's go play in the mud."

"Okay," said Albert.

They ran over to the muddy dirt pit and jumped in. Mud splattered everywhere.

"Stop it, guys!" said Joshua. "We're playing a birthday game here!"

"Watch this!" said Brendan as he began to dance. "This is called the silly mud dance." He stuck out his tongue and waved his arms. As he jumped all around, Brendan chanted, "Silly willy, muddy fuddy! Silly willy, muddy fuddy!"

Everybody laughed . . . even Danielle.

"Now it's *my* turn," said Tara. "I'm going to do a grouchy mud dance." Tara bent her knees, made a frown, and jumped from side to side.

The other children all took turns doing different mud dances. Finally, Danielle got off her swing and walked over to the muddy dirt pit.

"Can I dance, too?" asked Danielle in a soft voice.

"Of course!" said Tracy.

"What kind of dance do you want to do?" asked Joshua.

"A shy mud dance," replied Danielle.

Danielle tiptoed into the mud. *This feels pretty good,* she thought. Danielle did a slow, spinning dance.

After a while, she began to dance faster and faster.
"Now it's a happy dance!" said Danielle as she jumped
up and down with a big smile on her face.

When her dance was over, the other children cheered.
Danielle smiled. Then she looked down at herself.

"Uh-oh," said Danielle. "I've turned into a messy mud pie. Now I'm in trouble."

"Don't worry," said Mrs. Dee. "Look what I've got."

While Mrs. Dee cleaned her off, Danielle sang a new song:

I love mud, messy mud,
Alone or with my buddies.
I wish that it rained every night.
It's fun to get so muddy!